Contents

Legends at sea

Legends, or stories, tell us that sailing has often been full of adventure and excitement. But it can also be dangerous. How much do you know about shipwrecks? Can you tell if these sentences are true or false?

Angry whales have attacked and wrecked some ships.

Creatures called **Sirens** sing to trick sailors into crashing onto rocks.

Ships always sink during shipwrecks.

Many shipwrecks have never been found.

Legends of the Sea

Shipwrecks

Adrian Vigliano

www.raintreepublishers.co.uk
Visit our website to find out more information about Raintree books.

To order:
☎ Phone 0845 6044371
🖷 Fax +44 (0) 1865 312263
⌨ Email myorders@raintreepublishers.co.uk

Customers from outside the UK please telephone +44 1865 312262

Raintree is an imprint of Capstone Global Library Limited, a company incorporated in England and Wales having its registered office at 7 Pilgrim Street, London, EC4V 6LB – Registered company number: 6695582

Edited by Rebecca Rissman, Nancy Dickmann, and Siân Smith
Designed by Joanna Hinton Malivoire and Ryan Frieson
Original illustrations © Capstone Global Library 2010
Illustrated by Mendola Ltd
Picture research by Tracy Cummins
Production control by Victoria Fitzgerald
Originated by Capstone Global Library Ltd
Printed and bound in China by CTPS

ISBN 978 1 406216 21 9 (hardback)
14 13 12 11 10
10 9 8 7 6 5 4 3 2 1

ISBN 978 1 406216 26 4 (paperback)
15 14 13 12 11
10 9 8 7 6 5 4 3 2 1

British Library Cataloguing in Publication Data
Vigliano, Adrian
Shipwrecks. – (Legends of the sea)
910.4'52-dc22
A full catalogue record for this book is available from the British Library.

Acknowledgements
We would like to thank the following for permission to reproduce photographs: akg-images pp.**8**, **9**, **14**, **22**; Corbis p.**11** (© Reuters/Fabrizio Bensch); Getty Images pp.**13** (Michael Poliza), **15** (Steve Bloom), **24** (National Geographic/Pierre Mion), **25** (Time & Life Pictures) istockphoto p.**28** (LindaMarieB); Photolibrary p.**16** (Oxford Scientific (OSF)/Howard Hall); Shutterstock pp.**6** (© Petr Bukal), **7** (© Andrew Jalbert), **21** (© Jurgen Ziewe), **23** (© Scott Rothstein), **26** (© Durden Images); The Art Archive pp.**12** (Eileen Tweedy), **18** (Victoria and Albert Museum London / Sally Chappell), **20** (Ocean Memorabilia Collection); The Bridgeman Art Library International p.**19** (Percy Robert (1856-1934) / © Atkinson Art Gallery, Southport, Lancashire, UK).

Every effort has been made to contact copyright holders of any material reproduced in this book. Any omissions will be rectified in subsequent printings if notice is given to the publisher.

Some words are shown in bold, **like this.** You can find out what they mean by looking in the glossary.

Read this book to find
out the answers!

Shipwrecks

Ships are always in danger at sea !
A shipwreck happens when a ship
sinks into the water. A shipwreck can
also happen if a ship becomes stuck
on rocks or sand.

DID YOU KNOW?
There are thousands of wrecked ships in the world's oceans!

Siren shipwrecks

The ancient Greeks thought that ships had to watch out for creatures called **Sirens**. When sailors heard the Sirens singing, they would steer their ships towards the Sirens. But this was a mistake! The Sirens would lead the boats onto dangerous rocks.

Many stories say that Sirens had wings like birds.

IS IT TRUE?

There really were Sirens many years ago.

Answer: false

Build a good ship!

When ships aren't built well, they don't last long. In 1628, a **warship** called the *Vasa* only sailed for a few minutes. Then it tipped over and sank! It was carrying 150 men. When the *Vasa* was found the bones of 25 men were still in the ship!

The *Vasa* can now be seen at the Vasa Museum in Sweden.

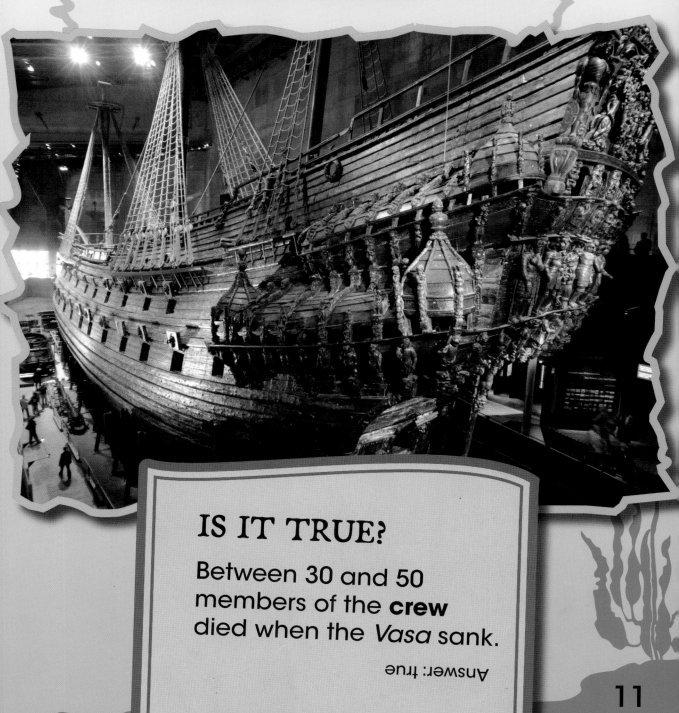

IS IT TRUE?

Between 30 and 50 members of the **crew** died when the *Vasa* sank.

Answer: true

Stay on course!

Sailors have many skills that help them to find their way. Many shipwrecks happen when a captain gets lost and makes a bad decision. A wrong turn at sea can lead a ship onto a deadly **coral reef**, or a rocky **coast**.

desert

DID YOU KNOW?

Can a ship sink in a desert? No, but a ship can sink in a sea and a sea can dry up!

Ships' graveyards are areas near **coasts** where many ships sink. Storms, fog, and rocks make ships' graveyards risky places to sail. Sailors use **lighthouses** to try to find a safe way through.

Ships' graveyards can be dangerous places to sail even after a storm is over.

lighthouse

Giants of the sea

In 1820 a ship called the *Essex* was hunting whales in the Pacific Ocean. Suddenly, a giant whale smashed a hole in the ship's side.

sperm whale

The ship sank and the **crew** of 21 sailors escaped in three tiny lifeboats.

When the men on the boats ran out of food, they had to kill and eat each other! Only eight members of the **crew** lived until help came – almost 100 days later.

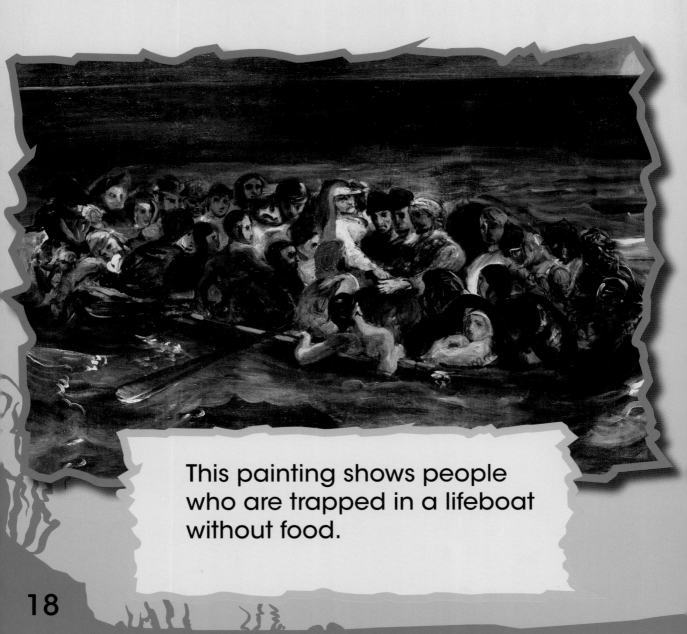

This painting shows people who are trapped in a lifeboat without food.

IS IT TRUE?

Shipwreck survivors can live for longer without food than they can without water.

Answer: true

Unsinkable?

In 1912 the *Titanic* was the biggest passenger ship in the world. It was built with an extra-strong **hull**. The hull is the main body of a ship. It could carry over 3,500 people. But on its first trip, the *Titanic* hit an **iceberg**.

Titanic

iceberg

The *Titanic* crashed into an iceberg like this. A huge part of the iceberg is hidden under the water.

The **iceberg** tore a hole in the side of the *Titanic*. The huge ship slowly sank into the freezing water. Passengers tried to find lifeboats, but there weren't enough for everyone. Over 1,500 people died when the *Titanic* sank.

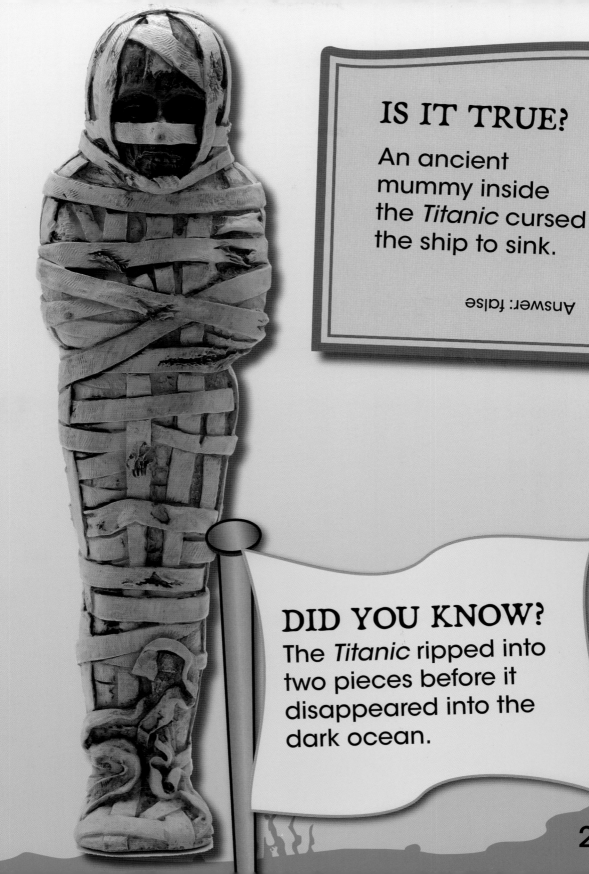

IS IT TRUE?

An ancient mummy inside the *Titanic* cursed the ship to sink.

Answer: false

DID YOU KNOW?

The *Titanic* ripped into two pieces before it disappeared into the dark ocean.

Finding shipwrecks

Many shipwrecks are never found. Even a ship as famous as the *Titanic* was lost for years. Scientists had to dive down 4 kilometres to reach it. That's about as deep as 730 giraffes on top of each other!

Finding the *Titanic* was exciting news. This painting shows the ship being explored.

DID YOU KNOW?

Scientists rode in a tiny submarine called a **submersible** to explore the *Titanic*. It was called *Alvin*.

Shipwreck hunters

Treasure hunters and scientists love to explore underwater shipwrecks. Studying old shipwrecks can teach people about the past.

Shipwrecks can be full of mysteries and surprises, such as gold coins and skeletons!

Learn to talk about a ship

Can you match the parts of a ship with what each name means?

① Stern

② Poop deck

③ Hatch

④ Helm

⑤ Bow

(a) Opening that leads to the lower levels of a ship.

(b) The back part of a ship.

(c) The raised area at the back of a ship.

(d) The front of a ship.

(e) A ship's steering wheel.

Glossary

coast the edge of land that is near water

coral reef sharp, jagged area in the water, often just below the surface. Coral reefs are made by tiny animals.

crew group of people who work on and run a ship

hull main body of a ship. The hull includes the ship's bottom, sides, and deck.

iceberg large, floating chunk of ice

legend story that started long ago

lighthouse tower with a bright light inside, used by people on the shore to help guide ships to safety

Sirens three creatures with wings and beautiful voices. The Sirens are characters from ancient Greek stories.

submersible tiny submarine, usually used to explore or do research underwater

warship ship that has weapons and is built for fighting

Find out more

Books

100 Facts: Shipwrecks,
Fiona MacDonald
(Miles Kelly Publishing, 2010)

Adventures in the Real World: Doomed Ships - Shipwrecks, Ghost Ships and Abandoned Vessels,
Penny Clarke (Book House, 2009)

Amazing History: Shipwrecks, Stewart Ross
(Franklin Watts, 2007)

Websites

www.nmm.ac.uk/explore/sea-and-ships/facts/
ships-and-seafarers/the-titanic
Find out all you need to know about the *Titanic*.

www.shipwreckcentral.com/map/index.
php?search=0&large=1
The map on this website shows you where shipwrecks have happened all around the world. Click on the dots to find out more about each shipwreck.

www.youtube.com/watch?v=6Z7REEnwKOQ
See the wreck of the *Titanic* for yourself in this underwater video.

Find out

Where did the *Titanic* sink?

Index